Daddy Was A Rock Star

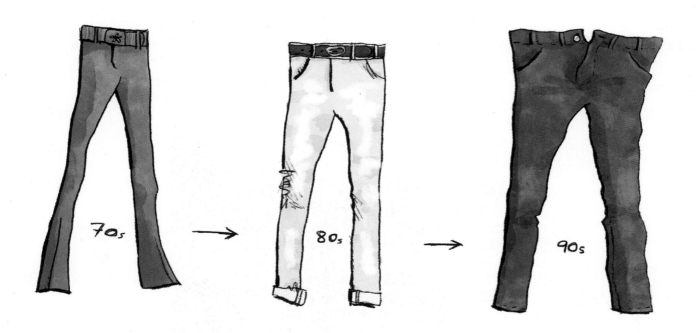

70s → 80s → 90s

For Paschal, Jeaic and Maeve.
Thank you for all your love,
encouragement and inspiration.

Text copyright: © 2022 Rosie Alabaster
Illustrations copyright: © 2022 Rosie Alabaster

www.rosiealabaster.com

ISBN: 9798408903672

Daddy Was A Rock Star

written and illustrated
by Rosie Alabaster

On the way to school one morning Eddie blurted out:
"My daddy was a **rock star**. I've only just found out!"
Some older kids were quick with a sneery, mean response
"He isn't anymore" jeered Jake "he just. Was. Once."

Eddie scuttled into class and kept his head down low.
When people think your dad is dull it comes as quite a blow.
He worried in his maths class, still fretting at home time.
Irked by what they'd said. Is old and wrinkly **such** a crime?

"How was school my darling?" Ed sighed and gave a shrug.
Mummy-instinct kicked right in and she wrapped him in a hug.

"Don't listen to them Eddie. Dad really is quite cool,
He may like doing jigsaws and just snoring by the pool.
He may like basket weaving and making pots of jam
But when it comes to being with you, he is your biggest fan.

Once he had a jet plane to take him to each gig
He wore super skinny trousers (before he got too big).
Daddy loved to smash TVs and leave hotel rooms in a mess
but he paid for all the damage, that's something I **should** stress.

Watch out, Joni!
Whoosh
OTEL
CHELSEA
♫ Woke up, it was a Chelsea morning and the first thing... ♫

He went to crazy parties and stayed up 'til way past three..."

"But now he just sits and sighs, dunking biscuits in his tea."

"Well, one day he gave it up so that he could be with us.
  He said that he was tired of all the travel, noise and fuss."

That evening, as daddy served his famous lentil stew,
Ed asked about his old life with his bandmates and his crew:
"Daddy, aren't you bored being stuck at home with me?
Don't you miss the glitz and glamour when you're
cooking me my tea?

Assembly next day was how St Giblets could go green;
Growing veg, hedgehog homes and air that's nice and clean.
"We also want to raise some cash to get our power for free,
we'll stick panels on the roof to make some solar energy.
Does anyone have thoughts on how this could be done?"

Ed piped up "Dad could give a concert,
I'm sure it will be fun."
Jake called out "Not that wrinkly
rocker who does jigsaws!"
Ed was not put off "Why not?
It's for such a **brilliant** cause!"

Eddie's daddy wasn't sure.
It was all so long ago.

"Get the band together
and the tunes will start to flow!"

The band was more than happy
to raise money for the school.
It was just the excuse they needed
to prove they were still cool.

They dusted off their amps,

they purchased new drumsticks.

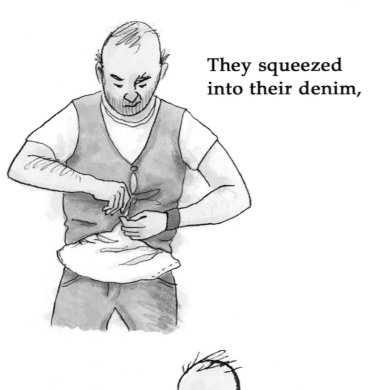

They squeezed
into their denim,

they practised
jumps and kicks.

On the day, the band forgot that they were old and bent.
They wowed the crowds with their greatest hits.
They **nearly** filled the tent!

The bassist got a little dizzy, tripped and took a knock
But overall, the gig was great and the crowd screamed;

YOU GUYS ROCK!!

In fact, the band raised so much money, they could buy a turbine too and now the school is eco-friendly, which I think's quite cool, don't you?

Ed loved hearing dad play in his heavy metal band
but he also felt a feeling for which he hadn't really planned:

He loved to see his daddy rock but was glad he'd settled down.
No longer touring round the world, moving from town to town.

Now dad was close at hand to pick Ed up from school.
To wipe his nose and fix his tea
and mess out in the pool.

Dad loves life more than ever now he's found the peace he sought,
leaving mummy time to do her job...

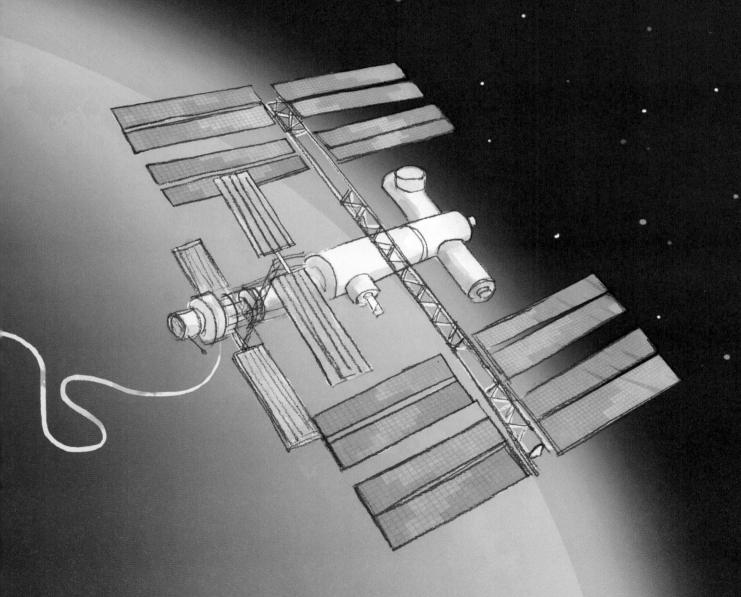

Printed in Great Britain
by Amazon